THE LOST HOUSE

A SEEK AND FIND BOOK

b.b. CRONIN

VIKING

Grandad promised to
take his grandchildren
to the park today.

—

But he needs some help
getting ready.

—

He's lost a few things.

In his green living room are seats, saucers, statues, and two socks.

Where are Grandad's socks?

In his shiny red kitchen, there are shelves full of dishes, a salt shaker,

and a tin full of sugar. But where are Grandad's shoes?

In his yellow bathroom, Grandad keeps his fishing tackle and his teeth.

He really can't go out without his teeth! Can you find them?

In the pink drawing room, there are pairs of galoshes and plenty of glass lamps.

There should also be a pair of Grandad's glasses in here. Where are they?

These are not
Grandad's glasses!

—

His are green.

They must be
in the living room.

—

Can you go back and
find them?

Grandad sees that it may start to rain. He will need an umbrella.

It's in this blue hallway—maybe by that pair of underwear or under that unstable table?

The orange sun is floating outside, but Grandad can't go out without his cloth tote bag.

It's not in the house, so it must be outside.

Grandad has almost everything, except for his pink-and-gray bow tie.

It might be here in his study full of books, banners, and one balloon.

In the purple reading room, time is ticking.

It's getting late, but where is Grandad's old pocket watch?

Grandad is sure he left his house keys up in the brown attic

with some kite string and a kettle. Where could they be?

While his grandkids look in the attic, Grandad looks in the green greenhouse for his hat.

His hat has a big hatband and a feather. Where might it be hiding?

In the magenta mezzanine, there are mirrors, mugs, and a mouse.

Grandad has two telephones. Where is his mobile phone?

Ready at last!

—

But where are
the kids?

Well,
he'll try again
tomorrow.

For Juliette, Henri, and Esmé

———

VIKING

An imprint of Penguin Random House LLC

375 Hudson Street

New York, New York 10014

First published in the United States of America by Viking,

an imprint of Penguin Random House LLC, 2016

LIBRARY OF CONGRESS CATALOGING-IN-PUBLICATION DATA IS AVAILABLE.

ISBN 978-1-101-99921-9

7 9 10 8 6

Manufactured in China   Set in Brandon Text

Book design by Mark Melnick